Published by Meadowcroft Publishing

Cover design by Book Cover Zone and Peter Boon.

Paperback cover by info@amapopico.com

Map of Chalk Gap Village

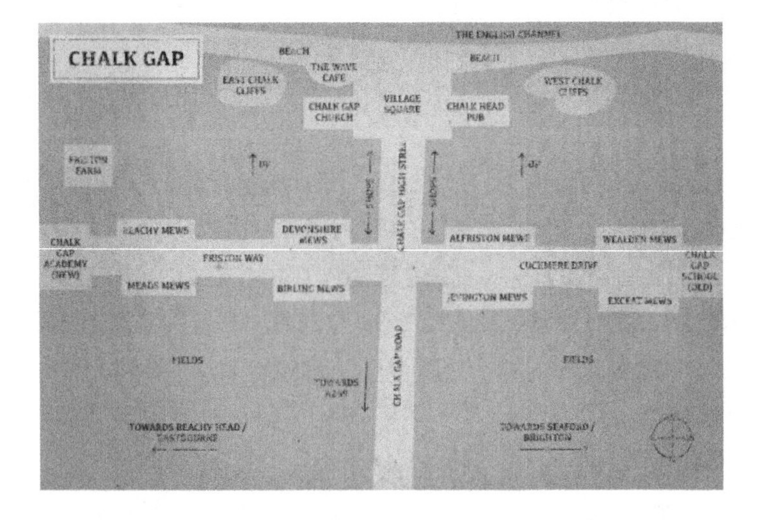

This summer themed book is the perfect one to dedicate to my dear friend, Adrian.

May the sun shine on you, always.

ECCENTRIC MULTI-MILLIONAIRE BRINGS NEW LUXURY HOTEL TO CHALK GAP... WHETHER WE LIKE IT OR NOT!

By Fiona Turtle

The controversial new luxury hotel on Chalk Gap seafront, Grande, is finally set to open next week after months of setbacks and public complaints.

Grande is owned by the eccentric multi-millionaire, Archibald Trent (better known as Archie), the older brother of Chalk Gap MP, Pierce Trent. It is not known who has been invited to the event at this point.

However, most locals are more concerned over the hotel itself, which is right next to Chalk Gap square and has been given its own private section of beach.

Local business owners are worried about the impact of the new venture. Proprietor of The Chalk Inn, Linda Crisp, said: 'This whole thing is a disgrace. Plonking his great big hotel next to our lovely square, what is he playing at? The types of people booking in there won't like our village, they'll be looking down their noses at us. It's no good for anybody.'

Village residents, meanwhile, are concerned about the 'private beach' directly in front of the hotel: meaning that non-guests won't be able to access that section of beach, being required to walk round it.

Pillar of the community, Linda, continued: 'So we

can't even access our own beach, how is that even legal? God knows who he bribed at the council to get away with that. Probably something to do with that MP brother of his.'

This isn't the first time that Archie Trent has caused controversy. He is notorious for bitter clashes with family members, employees and business rivals, although none could be reached for comment.

INVITATION

Dear Edward, Noah and Fiona

You are cordially invited to the private VIP opening of Grande on 17th August.

The event will be murder mystery themed with details given on arrival. Please be here for 4PM.

You are also requested to stay overnight. Luxury accommodation, evening meal and breakfast will be provided.

Please bring your brains and an overnight bag!

Yours kindly

Archibald Trent

1

'Oh wow, this is perfect! I can't wait.'

'We're not going, Noah.'

As soon as I saw the words 'murder mystery themed,' I knew that it was game over. There was no way my overly enthusiastic foster brother would take no for an answer now. Having moved on from his phase as a trainee journalist, he was now firmly back on the track of being a detective, though this time not just as an amateur; he now had ambitions to eventually become a fully-fledged police detective. I hoped this would make him ease off on the amateur stuff; I'd had more than my fill of murders over the last year and was hoping to take a break from it while we were enjoying our summer holiday break from Chalk Gap Academy (where Noah was a student and I worked as a school librarian). But apparently not.

'Of course we're going, don't be silly. There's no one better suited to solving a murder mystery event than us!'

I grimaced as he spoke, though I wasn't sure if that was due to his comment, or the uncomfortable feel of the hard pebbles beneath the towel I lay on.

Noah, Fiona, Mum and I were having a day on the beach. But, not just any old day on the beach. Mum and Fiona were combining our trip with a spying mission on Archie Trent's private beach, which was still under construction, meaning we were effectively sunbathing next to a building site.

And Mum was always fussy about which beach she'd go on, these days. We had a lovely resident of Chalk Gap, Adrian, who went along our beaches throughout summer to pick up all the litter left by beachgoers. He did a wonderful job and made a real difference to our village beaches. Mum's problem was he often did that job naked. 'I don't want to catch an eyeful from the Naked Litter Picker when I'm sunbathing.'

As for me, for someone who's lived most of his life with the seaside on his doorstep, I'm not particularly the beach-going type. I do like going for a swim in the sea, immersing myself in the cool, crystal water and being separated from the world for a while.

But right now, it was Noah in the sea and I was on shore. I shouted in reply to him, 'I think we've solved enough mysteries for a couple of amateurs, don't you?'

'Sorry, I can't hear you, I'm too far out!'

I lifted my head up to see that he was, in fact, getting further out to sea.

'But we've not had a mystery for months!'

So much for not hearing me. But as he continued to move away from us, he probably wouldn't hear me much longer.

'Please be careful in the sea! I think you should

come back now.' Noah maybe couldn't hear Mum from how far out in the water he was, but me and my eardrums certainly could.

Mum is always very over protective of Noah. Maybe it's because we've only been fostering him for little over a year (I always say 'we' even though technically it's just Mum and Dad), or maybe it's because of 'his special ways', as Mum calls them (the rest of us call them by their diagnosis, which is autism). Or maybe it's just the way she is; I remember her being the exact same with me and Alfie. In fact, she arguably still is. Either way, with Noah now being nearly 18, maybe she needed to relax a little.

'But Linda, I thought I saw a dead body floating, I need to check.'

Okay, maybe she had a point. Noah's fixation with dead bodies and murders had been known to get him in trouble before (although he was right on a few occasions too).

He was worryingly far out now, so much so that we could only just hear his matter of fact tone drifting across the open sea to us, and could only just make out his head bobbing up and down amongst the waves in the deep, choppy water.

'Edward, do something, he's way out of his depth! Go after him.'

I'm notorious for not being able to react quickly enough in a crisis. Everyone says I've got much better at it in the last year or so, but I'm not so sure.

'Noah, come back, please!' I shouted meekly as I stood at the edge of the sea.

'I could have done that myself,' Mum snapped as she shot me a deadly look from across the pebbles.

You could also go in after him, seeing as you taught me to swim, I wanted to say back, but I didn't.

'It's a body, Edward!' Noah hollered back.

'Noah, bodies don't float, they sink!' I replied in the loudest voice I could.

'Oh actually, it's just a burst inflatable,' I heard him reply, just as a particularly brutal wave covered him.

I'd now been joined by Fiona, my... I suppose you'd say my girlfriend, who gently put her arm around me as we both looked out to sea.

'Where is he, Edward, where is he?' Mum shrieked from behind us as she jumped to her feet.

It was a good question. I saw his head bob out of the water for a second before disappearing again. Was he in danger? And if so, what could I do about it?

Mum wasn't waiting to find out. 'Help! Help!' she screamed suddenly, making me jump a little. She continued her wails for help while I considered the situation. I spotted Noah's head pop up above the water before going under once more.

I don't do things on impulse very often, but this

was certainly one of those few times. Before I knew it, I found myself running into the water after him.

I remember feeling the cold first of all. It was a classic mediocre British 'sunny' day. Warm enough to sit on the beach in T-shirt and shorts, but probably not hot enough to go swimming (unless you're Noah). I shivered and tried to ignore the sudden change in temperature to focus on reaching Noah.

Next, I remember thinking that I should have stopped to take my T-shirt and denim shorts off. The sodden, soaking material clung to me, heavy and stubborn, as I tried to move forward.

Then, I felt pain under my feet as I hobbled across the stones under the water. Our beaches down here are pebbled, making them uncomfortable to walk on without footwear. Many people wear waterproof 'sea shoes' to go in the sea, but my impromptu rescue mission afforded me no such luxury.

From then on, I remember everything happening all at once.

'Be careful, Edward!' I heard Fiona shout behind me as I stumbled over a particularly large rock.

'Help!' I heard Noah splutter from in front of me.

'Go on Edward, get him, you can do it!' Mum again, though her next words, screamed at the top of her voice, contradicted her apparent faith in me. 'HELP!'

'Get back, get back!' This was an unfamiliar voice this time, as it took me a few seconds to realise someone was approaching behind me in the water. As I tried to step back to look, I felt a sharp rock under my foot, which caused me to lose my balance. I dropped backwards into the knee-high water, just in time to see a muscular figure in red shorts wade past me.

'I'll take it from here,' the mystery man said to me as he started to swim towards Noah. 'Get yourself back to safety.'

'Oh, what a hero!' I heard from behind me. Thankfully, this came from Mum not Fiona, which made me feel slightly less emasculated.

'Edward, come back and let a real man save him!' Thanks Mum, that will do it.

'I'm here, I'm here!' I heard Noah splutter as I got myself back to my feet. The unknown saviour was now swimming and he soon reached his target. He disappeared under a particularly scary looking wave for a second, but re-emerged pulling Noah to safety.

'Thank God, thank God!' shouted Mum, who was only ever religious when it suited her. I'd stumbled back to shore by now and Fiona ran straight to me, enveloping me in a hug.

A few seconds later, the mysterious man emerged from the water with Noah over his shoulder, before placing him carefully on to a beach towel. 'There you go, fella, easy does it.'

I took in the topless man's appearance for the first time. He was all bulging muscles and biceps; Mum was blatantly staring at him and I definitely spotted Fiona looking in his direction too. I looked at his wet, red swim shorts. While the women might have been looking at what was inside them, I noticed something written on the outside: *Grande Hotel.* Did the new hotel have its own lifeguard?

I put this thought to one side as attention focused on Noah. The lifeguard was doing CPR while Mum looked on anxiously. 'Is he awake? Say something, my darling!'

A moment or so after this, Noah spluttered and coughed himself awake, as the man stepped back from him. 'There we go, give him some space, everyone.'

Of course, Mum wasn't very good with the concept of space. 'Oh my darling boy, thank God you're alright!'

Noah opened his eyes and looked straight over at me. 'We're still going to the murder mystery evening at the new hotel, aren't we?'

2

'Okay, fella, I need to be absolutely sure you're okay before I leave you. So, one more time: how many fingers am I holding up?'

The unknown lifeguard had completely taken over the scene, his OTT alpha male energy pouring out of him.

Mum, increasing my embarrassment tenfold, was loving it. You would think she'd never seen a muscular man before, or didn't have Dad at home. 'Before you go, I must know the name of our hero.'

'His name is Tyler and he's my finest private lifeguard.'

We all turned to see Archie Trent standing there. I'd never met him personally, but I recognised him instantly; an expensive suit and fake smile of a man whose money couldn't buy him a younger age, despite all his efforts.

'What the hell are you doing here?' Mum snapped, as soon as she realised who it was.

'Ah yes, the lovely lady who's been giving me disparaging remarks in our finest local press.' He paused to glance at Fiona, who held his gaze defiantly. 'I think the question is, what are *you* doing *here*?'

'What, you own the whole beach now, do you?' Mum asserted quickly.

'Not the whole beach, but certainly part of it.

You're dangerously close to the private part of the beach that belongs to Grande Hotel. In fact, I think your foster son was nearly drowning in our section of the sea. Hence my lifeguard coming to save him.'

Mum whipped her head round to stare at said lifeguard, who looked away but smiled awkwardly. 'I haven't actually introduced myself. My name is Tyler.'

'He already told us your bloody name,' Mum snapped back, not even registering the hurt on the face of the man she was heaping praise on moments ago. She instead rose to Archie's bait. 'So, you think you own the sea now?'

The billionaire looked over his rounded glasses, perched on the end of his nose. 'Of course I don't own the sea, no one person can own such beauty. But I do have a contract giving my hotel exclusive use of that part of it. The area will be sectioned off by tomorrow.'

I could tell Mum was about to explode, but Fiona got there first with a thought I'd just had myself. 'How do you know Noah is Linda's foster son?'

Archie narrowed his eyes to take in Fiona, before falling into a huge, smug grin. 'I make it my business to know, Miss Turtle. Speaking of which, did you get my invite? I can't wait to welcome you all this weekend.'

'Yes, we can't wait,' an overly enthusiastic voice piped up from the pebbled ground.

'You can wait, Noah, and you'll have to,' Mum snapped. 'He can throw money round as much as he likes, but we won't be part of it.'

I could see that Archie was ready to bounce straight back with a response. I noted that he seemed to enjoy having a new sparring partner. 'But you're not part of it, Mrs Crisp. I'm sorry that the invite didn't include any *extras*. But I know that your son's curiosity, and that of his lady friend, will be too much for them to resist.'

I felt my cheeks flush red at the mention of me and Fiona. I was still processing my humiliation in the sea and Noah's near drowning; I didn't want to be brought into this argument.

However, Fiona knew how to reply. 'Thank you for the invite, Mr Trent. That discussion is, of course, a private matter and we'll let you know accordingly.'

'I'll let him know a few things right now.'

The fake smile on Archie's face dropped for the first time. 'Mrs Crisp, do be quiet. You may rule the roost in that neanderthal pub of yours, but you certainly don't with me. Come, Tyler.'

With that remark, he turned to leave with Tyler following him, the pebbles crunching beneath their feet.

Mum's face lit up with incandescent rage as Fiona held her back from following them. 'None of you will set a single foot inside that man's hotel.'

3

'I can't believe you're setting foot in that man's hotel.'

'Mum, it will be alright, I promise.'

To be fair, I hadn't wanted to go. Noah, of course, had been talking about nothing else other than going to a murder mystery evening. I thought Fiona would have sided with me, but her journalistic intrigue had got the better of her.

'Like I said, it's much better to know what we're up against in detail. Keep your enemies close, and all that.'

'Hmmm, I suppose so,' Mum muttered as she placed collected glasses into the glass washer behind the bar. 'I still can't believe he called this place a neanderthal pub.'

'He's got a point, love,' Dad said as he kissed her on the cheek. 'But it's *our* neanderthal pub and he can't take it away from us.'

'He bloody would, if he got the chance. He'd buy this whole village. Private beach and saying he owns the sea, who does that man think he is?'

'Linda, don't worry,' Fiona reassured her. 'Once we know a bit more about his hotel, we can make a plan.'

The plan was, as far as I knew, to gather enough information on Archie Trent to write an expose in Fiona's newspaper, thus putting enough pressure on the council to reverse their decision about the private beach. I just didn't think we needed to play along with his murder mystery game to do that.

But someone certainly did. The door from the pub flat pushed open and an overly large suitcase appeared in the doorway, with Noah peeping out from behind it. 'I'm ready to go!'

Mum's eyes almost rolled out of her head. 'Why on earth are you taking all that with you? Didn't it say just an overnight bag?'

'Yes, but there are certain essential items you need for a murder mystery event. In here I've got pens, flipchart paper, post-it notes, a magnifying glass, walkie talkies...'

We all exchanged a look but Fiona took this one. 'Noah, why would you ever need walkie talkies? We'll have our phones with us and we're only there one night.'

'You never know what the murderer might do to stop us communicating with each other. It's just a precaution.'

'It's all a publicity stunt anyway. I still don't understand why he's invited you,' Mum said.

'Because there's going to be a murder!' Noah said with his usual enthusiasm.

And he turned out to be right.

4

'Welcome to Grande Hotel.' Charley, the hotel manager (so her name badge said), smiled as she greeted us, but I sensed a hint of sadness underneath it. She was probably mid-thirties, a fairly broad and tall woman, and looked quite nervous, but had a pretty face and a sense of style I knew Fiona would love.

'You must tell me where you got that purple trouser suit, I love it!'

I grinned to myself at being right and noticed that Charley smiled fully this time in appreciation, with no hidden sadness. 'I'd love to. I'll tell you while I show you to your room.'

We'd been given a family room with Noah too, which was fine with me; my new relationship with Fiona hadn't yet included sharing a bed together, so it wasn't something I had to worry about that evening.

As we were led through the hotel, I noticed how nouveau riche everything was: shiny gold animal statues lay in the corridors, while neon colours adorned the walls.

'Archie Trent may be rich but he has no taste,' Fiona remarked, reading my mind. 'What do you think, Charley? Do you like the décor?'

The hotel manager looked flustered for a second, but a professional smile soon came to her face as she answered politely. 'Mr Trent chose everything personally, he took pride in it.'

The questioned unanswered, I knew Fiona wouldn't leave it there. 'It's not to your personal taste, then?'

Charley managed a shy grin. 'I guess it isn't what I would have chosen. Anyway, here's your room.'

'One more thing,' Fiona persisted. 'You've worked for Mr Trent before, haven't you?'

Charley turned a definite shade of red this time. 'Erm... briefly, yes. Anyway, I must be going.'

As she hurried down the corridor, it was Noah's turn for a question. 'Excuse me, what time does the murder start?'

She turned her head briefly to speak over her shoulder. 'The details should be in your room. See you later.'

'What was that about?' I asked as we entered our room, which was as gaudy and fluorescent as the rest of the hotel.

'I know, I only wanted to know what time someone's getting murdered. It's not too much to ask.'

'Not that, Noah.' I turned to Fiona, who was busy checking out the room. 'What was all that about? Why were you asking about Trent?'

'Just something I'd heard. Remember we're not here just for a free overnight stay. I want to find out what I can about Trent and how he's got away with this private beach business.'

'And we're here to solve a murder too.'

Fiona laughed to herself as she fell back on to the bed. 'That too, Noah. But I heard a rumour that Archie Trent's used previous employees and friends for all the positions in the hotel. Which is weird, because he's well known for having lots of issues with past staff.'

I realised where she was going with this. 'So, if these are the same people, why would they come and work for him again?'

She sat back up with excitement. 'Exactly. And Charley is one of those people, I did my research on her. She was the manager of his big Brighton hotel a few years ago and walked out, alongside several others.'

'And now someone's going to murder him!'

We both stared at Noah, who was holding a black A5 card in front of him. He repeated his words, much more dramatically this time. 'And now someone's going to murder him.'

He offered the card for me to read.

Dear detectives

I hope you don't mind me borrowing your brain power to solve a murder. MY murder.

Everyone here, except the three of you, have a reason to want me dead. I expect one of them has followed through with it.

By the time you read this, I'll probably be dead already.

Please make your way to the private lounge to start solving my murder.

Yours,

Archibald Trent

Noah picked up a rucksack from within his large case, and ran towards the door. 'Yes, the game has started! Let's go!'

As I went to follow him, I had a horrible feeling that this was more than just a game.

5

The lounge was a large, sparse room with three or four grouped sofa areas. The furniture was lime green, and a few bright, floral paintings hung on the walls, but otherwise the room was decidedly less gaudy than elsewhere in the hotel. It reminded me of a reception or lounge area of a Mediterranean holiday resort, and I decided that this must have been the look they were going for. I noticed a large projector screen on one of the side walls, while floor length dark curtains flapped in the wind on the back wall, evidently leading to some form of open terraced area.

The first thing I saw was a girl, probably about sixteen, wearing AirPods, sitting on a sofa engrossed in her smartphone as you might expect a teenager to be. But she seemed to give a sense of melancholy that you might not expect; she stared at her phone so intently, and so sadly, as if looking up from it might cause her world to implode. Her hair was short and dyed bright pink, while wearing a white T-shirt with the name of a band I can't remember. I noticed a little resemblance to Archie Trent, so I knew she must be related to him somehow.

Next to her was a middle aged woman, probably the girl's mother. She wore large sunglasses, despite now being indoors, and clutched her designer handbag as if she was afraid of someone stealing it from her. She was an obviously wealthy women who gave the air of being a class above those around her.

Just as I had this thought, Fiona whispered in my ear. 'That's Pierce Trent's wife, Wendy, and daughter, Natalie.'

Of course. Which must make the man in the corner of the room our local MP and Archie Trent's brother. I could see the similarities, though he was a bit younger. I'd seen his picture before but couldn't remember what he looked like: a slightly overweight man in his fifties trying to ignore his receding hair and middle aged spread. His voice boomed across the room as he spoke loudly on his phone. 'I thought we'd signed off on that? I need it on my desk by close of play today. Yes, I know it's the weekend.'

Wendy Trent finally noticed us and gave us a half smile. 'He can never switch off. But his work is so important for the community.'

I noticed how she didn't bother introducing any of them, having just presumed that everyone knew exactly who they were. She immediately turned away again, giving Fiona an opportunity to whisper more gossip.

'Oh, he's such a pillar of the community. You must remember the story about his daughter, Natalie.' She looked at me waiting for a response, before realising that I didn't. 'He had a scandal a couple of years ago for allegedly claiming her private school fees on MP expenses.'

Yes, that sounded familiar. But I didn't have too

long to dwell on it; I noticed too late that Noah was sitting down to join the family. Completely oblivious to Natalie wearing AirPods, he started speaking to her. 'So, who do you think will murder your uncle?'

He waited a few seconds before repeating the question in a louder volume. 'Who do you think will murder your uncle?'

Wendy Trent rolled her eyes. 'They can't hear you, young man, they're miles away as usual.'

Noah looked over at Wendy. 'Oh, she can't hear me? Should I tap her on the shoulder?'

Suddenly, Wendy stood up and snapped at Noah. 'Excuse me, did you just assume their gender? They use *they/them* pronouns.'

Noah doesn't always get social stuff but he is clued into modern gender issues. 'Oh sorry, I didn't know she was *they*. Oops… I didn't know *they* were they. Sorry, Natalie.'

'Oh, here we go, another one assuming they know my daughter because they've seen them in the press. Their name is Nat, actually.' She was making quite a scene now, so much so that Nat removed their AirPods, looking puzzled, and Pierce Trent started to end his call. Fiona and I stood by.

'I'm sorry for misgendering you, Nat.' Noah smiled and they smiled back. 'And sorry, Mrs Trent, but I don't know Nat from the press. We went to primary school together in Eastbourne. And they follow me on Instagram, but maybe I don't follow them back because I don't remember seeing anything about gender or being called Nat now.'

'Well, yes, Nat identifies as non-binary so please try and get their pronouns right in future.'

Nat herself now interjected, looking embarrassed. 'Mum, please, it doesn't matter. Stop making a big deal of it. I know Noah and he's lovely, he wouldn't do it on purpose.'

Pierce joined the conversation now, a blatantly public-facing smile on his face. 'See, dear, an old friend of Nat's. No harm done. And always nice to meet some of my constituents.'

He smiled at us all now, as I thought that Noah might just have gotten away with it. But he hadn't finished.

'Excuse me, Mrs Trent. You told me off for misgendering Nat, but you did it too.'

'I beg your pardon?' Her face was a picture of disbelief.

Noah smiled at her innocently as he continued. 'You referred to Nat as your daughter. But that's a female term, so if Nat is non-binary then you just misgendered them as female.'

I saw the pure rage form on Wendy Trent's face. Nat stifled a giggle while Pierce was quick to act, ushering her away to another sofa across the lounge. 'Let's sit over here, dear, and wait for my brother to arrive. Lovely to meet you all.'

Noah and Nat chatted casually about the horrors of the hotel décor as Wendy and Pierce argued in the corner. I couldn't help but hear some of their conversation.

'Look, dear, you know I respect Nat's choices but you need to lay off the heavy-handed gender stuff. You know my voters don't like all that far left mumbo jumbo.'

'Oh of course, here we go. Prioritising politics over your own family, typical. And as if you don't respect our child's chosen gender.'

'Darling, that's not what I'm saying -'

'You just want Nat to be a girl, don't you? You're getting as bad as that bigoted brother of yours, with his transphobic comments.'

'That was a long time ago he said those things, and it was probably exaggerated by the press anyway. He clearly doesn't think like that now. You know he worships Nat.'

As their conversation turned to Archie and therefore more interesting, a comment from Nat pulled me away from listening. 'Sorry about my parents. They mean well, I promise, but they're both... kind of idiots.'

Fiona and I laughed at this, the tension broken. 'You seem like a very smart young person anyway. I'd love to interview you for a gender article for my newspaper sometime.'

'Ugh, no offence but I'd hate that,' Nat replied

lightly. 'Being non-binary is no big deal, really. Just something I identify with. It's personal to me so I appreciate it when people try to get it right, but I don't have a stick up my arse about it like Mum does.'

'Your mum has a stick up her bottom? That must be uncomfortable.'

Luckily, we were interrupted before anyone had to respond to Noah. Charley, the hotel manager, and Tyler, the lifeguard who saved Noah, entered with a small group of others. Tyler had the same shorts on as before, but now with a tight-fitting yellow polo shirt instead of being topless. As I noticed Charley's anxious expression, I took in the other three people in the group. There was a tiny, sweet looking lady who must have been seventy-five at least, but was evidently still working despite her age: she was dressed in a smart, blue housekeeper's uniform.

Two men stood behind her, both looked around early thirties. One, from his attire, was clearly the hotel chef. He seemed very friendly, with a big smile on his face, but looked a little world worn: bags under his eyes, thinning hair and skinnier than you might expect a chef to be. The other man, wearing a smart white shirt and black waistcoat which appeared to be a bar staff uniform, looked decidedly less friendly as he scowled around the room. He was also much shorter; he couldn't have been more than five foot five.

Charley spoke first. 'Ah, okay. Sorry folks, I think there's been a mix-up. We're using this room for our staff meeting.'

Pierce Trent was straight on his feet, waving his black invite card that was probably the same as ours. 'No, we've been told to come here. Look, what's going on? Where's my brother?'

The scowling barman stepped forward. 'Somewhere playing games with us, it looks like.'

Charley stepped forward and gestured to Pierce to pass her the card. 'That's odd. This isn't the original invite we put in rooms. It had a different meeting time and place. And it didn't say anything about Mr Trent himself being the murder victim. That was supposed to be a surprise!'

Wendy Trent spoke next, somehow managing to acknowledge what Charley had said while simultaneously ignoring her. 'Come on darling, let's go. This sounds like one of your brother's stupid tricks.'

Just after she said this, the voice of Archie Trent himself filled the room. 'Hello, everyone. I'm sorry if there's any confusion.'

We all turned to greet him, but he wasn't there. Instead, there he was on the projector screen, sitting in a deckchair on what looked like one of the hotel balconies or terraces.

'Okay, then. Shall we get started?'

6

I couldn't help but be reminded of a Bond villain as we all watched Archie Trent on the large screen, speaking from his deckchair. He wore a Hawaiian shirt and matching shorts, had sunglasses on and held an exotic looking cocktail, complete with umbrella and all the trimmings

He'd barely spoken yet, but I felt that same sense of smugness from when we met him on the beach. He definitely seemed to be going all in on the drama of his murder mystery event.

'You may be wondering why you've been gathered here. And I don't just mean this room, I mean to this hotel in general. Most people in this room hate me. So, yes, you are all here for the sole purpose of my murder. But which one of you will it be?'

Noah jumped out of his seat with delight. 'Yes, who?' I noticed Wendy Trent roll her eyes while her husband nudged her.

Archie continued on the screen. 'Let me introduce you all to each other. Of course, most of you know my brother, Pierce Trent. With him is his *lovely* wife, Wendy, and their only child, Nat. I'm going to be honest: my brother and I have our differences, but Nat is the apple of my eye. I'm a very proud uncle to Nat and they should continue being whoever they want to be.'

The sarcasm in his voice in his description of

Wendy was palatable and, of course, she fumed at this. I guessed there was no love lost between the in-laws. More surprising was his comments about Nat, who he identified using their correct pronouns and seemed very fond of. This didn't seem to fit Wendy's comments about him a few moments ago.

'Next, let me introduce my staff. Ladies first. Charley is our hotel manager and is the best woman for the job. Again, someone I'm very proud of. She can speak four languages.'

I glanced over at Charley, who looked a little embarrassed, with her head down. 'Next, we have my housekeeper, Beryl. Then, we have my lifeguard, Tyler, my bar manager, Leon, and my chef, Breakfast.'

Wait, what? Noah beat me to it. 'Did he just say your name was *Breakfast*?'

The man in chef whites stepped forward, still smiling like before. 'Yeah, that's right. My name's Ash Brown, so they always call me Breakfast. Course, I had to become a chef after that.'

He grinned again as Tyler, the lifeguard, clapped him on the shoulders, the two laughing together. I noticed the bar manager shooting the pair an evil look, which made me wonder about the dynamics between the three men.

'Shush, the video's back on,' Beryl, the housekeeper, said to them in a direct but not rude manner. She was well spoken and delivered her words in a clipped manner.

'... and of course, not everything is as it seems,' screen Archie was saying. 'Everyone in this room has been given an opportunity. Because no-one is here by coincidence. Firstly, our well known local amateur detectives, Edward and Noah, along with local journalist, Fiona, who has taken more than a passing interest in my affairs lately, have the opportunity to solve my murder.'

I felt all eyes on us. Fiona, not fazed by the dig at her, smiled defiantly. I could tell Noah was about to speak but the bar manager, Leon, beat him to it. 'I'm getting bored of this. Why are we here?'

Right on cue, video Archie supplied the answer. 'The rest of you each have a reason for wanting me dead. I arranged for every single one of you to be here to achieve that purpose. Whether that be one of my family or one of my *staff*, you all have a past with me and you all hate me. By the time you see this, I'll be dead already, murdered by someone in this room.'

As I glanced round the room and took in the expressions on each face, I could feel the intense, uneasy atmosphere. This didn't feel like a murder mystery game. Something wasn't right.

And Archie wasn't finished. He leaned forward to the camera, brandishing an object which he waved in front of his face. It took me a couple of seconds to realise it was a silver dagger, sharp and menacing.

'Each person had a dagger exactly like this waiting

for them on arrival at the hotel today. Each staff member found it in their locker, while my brother and his family found theirs in their rooms on arrival.'

Archie's brother himself was the first to comment. 'Yes, and it was a very clever way to start this game. Though I'm not sure why we had real daggers. I guess whoever's been appointed the murderer had an extra note telling them that they did it. Which, of course, isn't me.'

'I don't think it's a clever way to play the game at all,' his wife remarked. 'I thought we'd all be given characters and profiles, not just playing ourselves.'

Again, on cue, when Archie spoke on the screen again, it was almost as if he was replying directly to them. 'This isn't just a game. All the suspects each have a very real reason to murder me, for real. And by the time you see this, I'll already be dead.'

The video cut off abruptly, leaving a blank screen while we all stared at each other.

'This is fantastic!' Noah said, somewhat predictably.

But I was already thinking ahead, knowing in my heart what we were about to find. I addressed the group of staff. 'That balcony, where is it?'

Charley, the hotel manager, answered immediately. 'I don't think it's a private room balcony, from the layout. It's too spacious. It looks like one of the conference suite balconies, but we have several. It could be any, although...'

Her voice tailed off as I followed her gaze to the back of the room, where the curtains flapped in the wind.

I knew instantly. 'It's the balcony of this room.'

Without thinking, I ran to the back of the room, Fiona and Charley following me.

And that's where we saw Archie Trent's body slumped in his deckchair, with a dagger in his back.

7

The dagger had cut straight through the deckchair and into Archie's back, leaving dark crimson blood stains on both. This was no joke or game; he was dead, for real. It was a few moments since I'd found the scene – I'd now stepped back inside the room – but I couldn't get the image out of my head. My heart was pumping and I felt sick.

I looked round the room at the shocked and upset faces. Not a word had been spoken yet but everyone knew what had happened. Fiona was comforting Charley, who'd been on the balcony with us. Noah had taken a notebook and pen out of his rucksack and was scribbling away.

Nat, only a teenager still and one of only two blood relatives in the room, cried quietly. Pierce looked solemn while his wife was completely poker faced. Beryl, the elderly housekeeper, looked terrified whilst the male staff all looked at the floor in disbelief.

'We need to call the police,' I said, as I reached for my phone. But, I was surprised to find I had no signal. Fiona and Noah checked their phones too, before everyone in the room followed in turn to discover the same thing.

'What the hell's going on?' said Wendy Trent, with panic in her voice.

'It's fine, I'll go down to reception and call from

there,' Charley replied. I could tell she was trying to keep calm and take charge, but I could see the horror in her face. She'd had the same chilling view on the balcony I'd had.

'Let's go then,' Tyler said, as he virtually sprinted to the door in his tight-fitting outfit, barely avoiding pushing past her. It reminded me of him wading past me in the sea to save Noah, desperate to be the alpha male. Perhaps it was his way of coping.

'That's strange,' he said as he repeatedly pressed the green 'push to exit' button. He took a staff fob from his pocket and tapped it against the sensor near the door. He looked over to Breakfast (I don't feel right calling him that, but that's how he'd introduced himself). 'You come try, fella.'

The chef did the same and had no luck. The other staff members all tried one by one, to the same effect.

'So we're trapped here... with a murderer!' Beryl almost screamed. I noticed for the first time how tiny and frail she looked, and wondered why she was still working as a housekeeper well past her retirement age.

'It's fine, we can get out from the balcony,' Tyler said as he bounded back to the other side of the room. He definitely saw himself as the action hero in this bizarre real life movie that was playing out in front of us.

'Tyler, remember we're on the twelfth floor and

there's no fire escape or other balcony near us,' Charley asserted, rolling her eyes.

He stopped suddenly, looking puzzled. 'Who would build a hotel like that?'

'A freak who wants to trap us all here with his dead body,' Leon, the scowling barman, said.

Pierce Trent stepped forward. 'Please have some respect for my dead brother.'

'Oh shut up, Pierce, he's right,' Wendy Trent said. 'Dead or alive, he obviously wants to play some sick game with us, as usual.'

'Stop it, all of you!' Nat shouted as their parents squabbled. 'Look, surely we can shout for help from the balcony.'

Charley shook her head. 'Sadly not. Again, we're on the twelfth floor and remember we're overlooking a private beach that no one can access. Mr Trent even increased the boundaries further yesterday, after he said he found intruders.'

Fiona and I shared a look; I was relieved Mum wasn't here to hear us being called that.

'No, it must be worth a try. Help! Help!' Tyler started calling as he strode out to the balcony, though he was back mere seconds later, looking pale. 'Erm, I kind of forgot there's a dead body out there. Maybe we'll think of something else.'

'Don't worry, I have everything covered. I was prepared for a situation like this,' Noah said, rummaging in his bag. 'Here, take this, Edward. At least we can communicate with each other.'

I looked at the object to see that he'd handed me a walkie talkie. 'What am I supposed to do with this? We're all trapped in the same room.'

'Oh yes,' he replied, looking puzzled, before hunting round in his bag again. 'Maybe we can use this magnifying glass to look for clues?'

'Maybe, Noah, we'll keep it in mind.' As I humoured Noah gently, I could feel the panic in the room rising.

'Who's doing this to us?' Pierce asked.

Wendy answered her husband bluntly. 'I think we know the answer to that.'

'And how is it even possible to trap us in a room with no phone signal or way out?' Pierce spoke in an almost childlike way, with no clue of the answer. It occurred to me that he was probably the kind of MP who had a team of people to make every decision for him.

'It's quite easy, actually. He must have installed a signal blocker in here or on this floor and had it on a timer. The same with the electronic door controls, he could have programmed them to lock down at a specific time.'

I was surprised that it was Beryl saying this, and it appeared everyone else was too as we all gaped at her, except teenage Nat, who looked impressed and nodded along in agreement.

'What? An old lady can't know about technology? I live on my own and I've been running my Smart Home Security System for a few years now. Don't stereotype me, please.'

'He can't have us all trapped. We'll have to break the door down,' Tyler said, probably keen to re-establish his masculinity after balking at the body.

'I'm afraid not,' Charley said. 'There's no budging them. I wondered why he insisted on having steel doors.'

Noah looked up from his notepad. 'So, yes, he has us all trapped! Until we solve his murder.'

Just as Noah spoke, the screen flickered on again before Archie appeared, still alive in his deckchair. 'This is a predicament, isn't it? Should I tell you what you have to do to get out? I hope you're all ready to put your trust in one person. Because it's all going to come down to our friend, Edward Crisp. No pressure, Edward.'

8

My anxiety shows itself in different ways. Sometimes I have panic attacks, where I struggle to control my breathing and need to ground myself again. On other occasions, I've laid awake all night over-thinking every possible scenario, or replaying something over and over again in my mind.

Then there's the kind of anxiety I have when I'm forced into a situation. I used to run; I remember locking myself in the pub toilet once when Mum tried to forcibly set me up on a date.

Being locked in a twelfth floor room with multiple other people including a murderer, running wasn't an option this time. Besides, I'd grown since then. One reason was solving multiple murders as an amateur, which had improved my confidence no end.

And the other reason was right next to me, holding my hand. Knowing that Fiona was with me, that she had my back and we were in it together, made me feel that I could tackle anything. Even a situation as bizarre as the one I was currently in.

'Edward, I've been very impressed with you in the last couple of years,' video Archie told us, as everyone around me looked increasingly frustrated and frightened. 'You may have noticed that I have a *penchant* for courting press attention. I crave it, if I'm being honest. But here's you; the shy, awkward amateur detective wanting a quiet life but constantly pushed into the spotlight. And I hear some reports say you're better than the police.

'It fascinates me. So, I decided to put you to the test, Mr Crisp. It's my time to leave this earth and I've decided to go out with a bang. In 60 minutes time, the door to this room will open and the police will arrive for what they think is a routine visit.

'Now, I want my killer to meet justice and I believe they will either way. But, will you be able to present the murderer to them when the time's up, or will everyone here be subjected to a long police investigation? Over to you, Mr Crisp. I'd say your first job is to uncover everyone's secret. Good luck. Oh, and by the way, there are clue prompts everywhere.'

The image on the screen disappeared as everyone looked dumbfounded.

'This is amazing! Let's get started,' Noah declared with excitement, before his expression changed to mild disappointment. 'Though he could have addressed it to both of us. We are a team, after all.'

Leon, the scowling barman, looked on in disgust. 'We're not actually going along with this, are we? Letting some amateur investigate us?'

Breakfast (yes, I'm reluctantly calling him that name) punched him on the arm as he laughed. 'Why not? Nothing to hide have you?'

I saw a look exchanged between the two men. 'Of course I haven't. But this is ridiculous. We need to find a way out of here, or if not, wait and let the police deal with it.'

Wendy Trent addressed her husband, who looked shaken. 'You can't afford the bad publicity of this. We need to get out of here.'

'Bad publicity? Mum, Uncle Archie is lying dead a few feet away from us. Don't you think Dad might be upset about it? It was his brother.'

'It's okay, pumpkin,' Pierce Trent sat down next to Nat and put his arm around them. 'Mum's just in shock, like we all are.'

'When we've quite finished with the family therapy, we need to get out of here,' Leon snapped.

Charley, the hotel manager, stepped forward now. 'Why do you have to be so rude? I don't know why Mr Trent hired you again.'

'Same reason he hired you and everyone else, to torture us.' He looked round the room, fixing his eyes on each person in turn. 'I think we can all agree that we hate the old bastard. And that's why we're all here.'

'He's right,' I heard myself say as I stepped forward. This wasn't the situation I wanted to be in, and I had no idea if I was doing the right thing or not, but my instinct had kicked in. 'I think we need to start with you all telling us the truth about your history with Archie Trent, and thus why you're here.'

'Yes!' Noah punched the air with delight, earning himself dubious looks from Wendy Trent and Leon.

‘I thoroughly agree,’ I heard a little voice say. I turned to see it belonged to Beryl, the elderly housekeeper. ‘We all must be honest about our secrets. And I’ll start.’

9

'I was Archie's personal housekeeper for many years. He trusted me and we were dear friends. But then it all went wrong.'

'Let me guess, little old lady housekeeper cliché number one. He caught you stealing the silverware,' Leon said, rolling his eyes.

'Oh no, not that. We were sleeping together.'

Several eyes in the room almost popped out of their head. Pierce Trent in particular looked horrified.

'What? I'm not *that* much older than him. Besides, a girl's got to get it where she can at my age.'

'You were clearly after his money,' Wendy Trent said through pursed lips. 'Number one suspect, I'd say.'

I wanted to keep Beryl focused before this descended into argument. 'What went wrong then, if you were in a relationship together?'

Beryl laughed out loud. 'Oh you young people and all your romance. We were literally just sleeping together. But yes, it did go wrong.'

'What happened?' Noah was the one to ask, but I could tell the elderly lady had the whole room's attention now.

'The sour-faced one is right. I *was* after his money. At first, anyway.' She took a moment to take in everyone's shocked reactions. 'What? An old girl's got to get by however she can. But it wasn't like that. I fell for him. And when he realised his money could get him much younger models than me, it broke my heart.'

'I'm sorry my brother did that to you.'

'For God's sake, Pierce. Grow a backbone and turn off your PC do-gooder routine for five minutes. You heard her, she was after his money.'

'Mum, don't be horrible. She just said Uncle Archie broke her heart. Have some empathy.'

'Thank you, dear,' Beryl said to Nat.

Something occurred to me. 'How did you get your revenge on him?'

Beryl turned to me and narrowed her eyes. 'What makes you think I did that, my dear? You know my motive. He broke my heart.'

But I wasn't convinced. 'From what I've learned about Archie, I don't think that's enough of a reason to bring you here. He had the upper hand. You must have done something to him after that, to be on his radar now.'

As I was talking, I noticed Noah had left his seat and was wandering around the room, probably looking for clues.

Beryl, meanwhile, dropped her sweet smile for the first time. 'You are a clever one, aren't you? Well, yes, there is a little more to tell, in fact. But I'm not sure if

I should say in front of the family.'

Fiona, who had been listening intently by my side, moved towards the old lady before she spoke. 'Look. I don't know what's happening here. But everything is clearly going to come out either way. If you're innocent of *this*, you need to help us get to the truth. And the only way to do that is to tell us what he has on you.'

I could almost see the thoughts in Beryl's head as she contemplated Fiona's words, before she eventually spoke. 'Oh, okay. I tried to burn his house down.'

Pierce Trent jumped to his feet. 'That was YOU?'

His wife almost looked impressed. 'I always thought it was one of those young, reckless models he was famous for dating.'

'Oh no, dear. They're the types he cast me aside for. But not on my watch.'

Leon, standing next to her and sneering in his immaculate uniform, spoke next. 'There we have it, our most likely suspect. She's already an arsonist.'

Beryl didn't miss a beat. 'Better an arsonist than just an arse.'

'I don't have to take that from an old bat like you.' He raised his voice now as he looked around the room. 'It's clear that she's the murderer. Let's just keep her here until the police arrive. It's clear the rest of us have done nothing wrong.'

'I'm not sure about that,' a voice called from across the room. I turned my head to see Noah waving a piece of paper. 'Look at this note I've found.'

I took it from him and read.

Everyone is here because I blackmailed them. Well, almost everyone.

10

Noah paced up and down the front of the room dramatically. 'Almost everyone! That gives everyone, apart from the one person or more who isn't being blackmailed, their motive.'

'And what about that person or persons?' Fiona joined in. 'Why are they here? Do they have a separate motive?'

'I think they *all* have a motive,' he replied.

'Hello? We are here, you know,' Wendy Trent snapped.

'Don't we know *you're* here,' Leon remarked. As the whole group joined in the bickering, I tried to think.

All (or almost all, apparently) of these people were being blackmailed by a man who now lay dead, merely feet away from us. One of them had murdered him and we'd already had one unlikely arsonist reveal themselves.

Who knew what other crimes were being hidden by the people I was trapped with? The sensible thing to do was hold out the remainder of the hour until the police came, and let them deal with it. Everyone would be interviewed and the correct person would be arrested, along with anyone else suspected of anything criminal.

But, that gave us a lot of what ifs. What if the murderer fled as soon as they were able? What if they managed to kill again while we were all trapped by them? Or, a little voice in my head was nagging me, what if I was the one who was meant to solve this mystery?

Archie Trent, no matter how bizarre his plan was, had requested me to solve his murder. There must have been a reason. Moreover, there must have been a reason why he was willing to be murdered in the first place.

Bringing all his blackmail victims into one place and handing them all a weapon, he was almost goading them into killing him: knowing that one of them would.

But why would you want to die? He was only recently 60, and with his wealth would have all the means to fight off the ailments associated with forthcoming old age.

Then, some of his words from earlier came flying back to me. '*My time to leave this earth.*'

Before I knew it, I was addressing the group. 'I have a theory. And I'm sorry if this is upsetting for any loved ones of Archie's here. But, has it occurred to anyone why he felt it was his time to leave this earth? He's barely 60, he had a successful life and career. Yes, he had his enemies, but he was a loved uncle at least. Why would he want someone to kill him?'

His brother spoke next, though he kept his eyes to the floor. 'My God, he was dying anyway, wasn't he?'

'I think it's a strong possibility,' I said in reply.

There was quiet for a moment as I tried to take in as many reactions as possible. I didn't know who yet, but amongst these people the murderer had just discovered that their victim was dying anyway. They'd been played by their blackmailer who had just ruined their life even further.

To be fair, no one particularly looked angry or guilty: everyone seemed either sad or shocked, or both. Even the more vocal people like Wendy Trent or scowling Leon didn't say anything. The room was silent.

I took advantage of this to continue addressing them. 'If this is the case, and Archie had nothing to lose, it appears that he's gone all out to target each of you, knowing that one of you would snap and kill him. We just need to figure out which one.'

'This is all just a big game to that guy,' Tyler said. This was the first time the lifeguard had spoken in a while.

'But what a game!' Noah said in reply, earning himself multiple dark looks.

'Of course it's a game,' I said. 'He's designed it as such. My presence here and what he said in the video shows that. We just need to play the game and win.'

'And what about the killer?' Charley, the hotel manager, asked. 'Will they be playing the game? Because we're trapped here with them and they'll be playing by different rules to us.'

'What choice do we have?' Fiona said. 'How do you know they're not going to strike again anyway? Or escape as soon as that door opens?'

'We are not seriously doing this,' Leon said with his now signature scowl on his face. 'Like I said, this guy is an *amateur*. Isn't he like a school secretary or something?'

'School librarian,' Noah said quickly.

'Whatever. Either way, I think I'll take my chances with the police, thank you very much.'

Pierce Trent stood up and looked at me, before smiling. 'I actually know a little about Edward Crisp and the work he's done with the police. He's virtually famous in my constituency. And I trust him to get to the bottom of this, especially as we are stuck here anyway.'

'We don't just have to do what this geezer says!' This came from Breakfast (I guess I'm using that name after all) who had moved closer to Leon, presumably to show his agreement with him.

'No we don't,' Fiona said. 'But seeing as we have an MP here anyway, why don't you be democratic and all vote? If the majority vote in favour, Edward will investigate. If the majority are against, we just wait for the police. Agreed?'

'I've already confessed my arson and I'm quite intrigued to see what everyone else has been up to. So let's get on with it,' Beryl said.

Everyone else nodded in agreement, to the vote at

least, so Fiona carried on. 'All in favour of allowing Edward to investigate you, raise your hand, please.'

Beryl's hand went straight up. Pierce and Nat Trent also raised their hands quite quickly, followed by Wendy after some eye contact between the three. They were finally joined by Charley.

'Those against? Raise your hand, please.'

The three male employees – Tyler, Leon and Breakfast – all shared a nod before each putting a hand up.

'And I wonder why you three don't want him investigating,' Charley said. I noted that for later.

'It doesn't matter, dear. The vote is 5-3 so we win. Time to hear everyone's secrets,' Beryl said with a sugar sweet smile.

'That's not what we voted on,' Wendy Trent said.

'It kind of is where we need to start,' I explained to her. 'Establishing why each one of you was blackmailed will help us.'

She turned and hit her husband's arm with the back of her hand. 'Great! Look what we voted for.'

'Now you know how his constituents feel,' Fiona said.

Ignoring this, Pierce replied to his wife. 'Look, we have nothing to be afraid of. My brother, God rest his soul, is dead out there and this story is going to be everywhere whether we like it or not. Let's get ahead of the story, and hopefully help catch whoever did this at the same time.'

I couldn't work Pierce out. He was likely in shock about his brother's murder, but he was definitely being more reasonable and more open than I expected.

'The reason for blackmailing us is simple,' he continued. 'You may remember the fuss about me allegedly paying for Nat's school fees through MP expenses. Totally untrue, of course. Nevertheless, my brother claimed to have proof of it and threatened to expose it every time he wanted something. Which, on this occasion, was coming here for this charade.'

Wendy patted his arm, while looking relieved. Was she expecting something else?

'Oh that's pretty handy,' Fiona remarked. 'Your secret's one that everyone already knew. I wonder why that is.'

I'd had the exact same thought. 'It doesn't seem right that he'd blackmail you about something that was common knowledge. Are you sure it wasn't something else?'

'No, it's all bullshit!' Nat shouted suddenly, jumping from their seat. 'Mum and Dad have so many secrets you could take your pick what it might be. They act like we all live these perfect lives, but we don't. It's bullshit!'

With that, Nat stormed past the curtain at the end of the room and out on to the balcony.

Wendy went to follow them. 'They're not safe out there. What about the dead body?'

Pierce put a hand on her to stop her. 'Leave her. She needs time to calm down. She'll be fine.'

'Oh yes, out there chilling with their uncle's corpse! And you just misgendered them. I know it's a stressful situation, but do take care, Pierce.'

I decided to move the focus away from the Trent family for now. They still had a secret (at least one), but now wasn't the time to pursue that. Besides, there was something else that had piqued my interest.

The three male hotel employees were all looking relieved that the attention was away from them after Charley's comment. But what was that about? They had all voted against me questioning them, and clearly had something to hide that involved all three. I decided to tackle this a different way.

Addressing the employees' group as a whole, I said, 'am I right in thinking you've all worked for Archie Trent before?'

As I'd predicted, Charley's eyes went right to the three men. 'Yes.'

'Why are you looking at us like that?' Leon asked her immediately.

'Yeah, chill,' Tyler said.

I didn't have to do much else, as Wendy Trent spoke up. 'What is going on with you three? You were the only three who didn't want Edward to question you, your colleague has alluded multiple times to something suspicious, and quite frankly, you all look dodgy as hell.'

'Oi!'

'Leon, she's right,' Breakfast said. 'It's all gonna come out anyway, we might as well just tell them.'

'With his family right there, and a journalist as well?' Leon said.

'I agree with Breakfast,' Tyler said. 'Charley's going to tell them all anyway if not.'

The three looked at each other, seemingly at stalemate. Beryl broke the silence. 'I've never worked in Archie's hotels, but it's obvious what's happening here. Leon, when I was telling my story as an ex-employee, your first thought was that I must have stolen something. Judging by your own standards, were you?'

'How dare you…' he started, standing up to square up to the old lady, before seemingly remembering himself.

'You could say that,' Charley chipped in. 'But this goes way beyond pinching a bit of silverware. These three ran a racket fleecing Mr Trent for thousands upon thousands. And they got away with it for years.'

I'd guessed it was something along those lines. The three had appeared conspiratorial since we'd been here. And Archie Trent blackmailing the men who'd stolen a fortune from him seemed right on brand. 'My guess is that when you were found out, rather than press charges, he let you all go and held it over you to use another time.'

'Like forcing me to come back here and watch idiot kids in their rubber rings for minimum wage,' Tyler said.

'You're pretty spot on,' Charley said to me. 'All three of them were quite high up in the company by the time they were found out. All skimming a fortune off the top.'

Okay, I didn't guess that bit right. The cocky lifeguard, the surly barman and the chirpy chef were actually way above that and presumably blackmailed into these roles now by Trent for one final humiliation.

'While you barely made it beyond a reception desk,' Leon said to her with a smirk.

'What can I say, it's a man's world,' she replied with a hint of bitterness.

'This doesn't make sense,' Pierce said. 'You're telling me that my brother let the three of you off from theft of a fortune, just so he could bring you back to embarrass you later? That's ludicrous.'

'That's your brother,' his wife remarked.

Just then, there was a crackle from the large screen and Archie Trent appeared in front of us once more.

'Hello again, everyone. Now, if my timing is correct we are about halfway through our time together here. So, time for a new clue.'

We all looked around at each other, no one knowing what to expect next.

'There's something about me none of you know. I had a son. And they're in this room right now. In fact, I expect they're probably the killer.'

11

Everyone in the room stared at the three male employees: Leon, Tyler and Breakfast. I observed that they were all probably around the same age: early thirties.

'That's right, go for the obvious,' Breakfast said first. 'What makes you think it's one of us?'

'Well, it's hardly me, is it?' Beryl said with her sweet smile.

There was a general sense of shock in the room. Pierce Trent looked especially shaken. Even Nat had returned from the balcony and stood in the doorway, looking gobsmacked. Wendy looked over to Nat to make eye contact, but they wouldn't meet her gaze.

Pierce fell back into his seat. 'You mean to tell me, that my brother had a son for all this time, and no one knew about it. Not possible. I would have known. I would have.'

'Maybe he only found out himself recently,' Beryl said, before she paused. 'I'm not the mother, by the way.'

'We know that, seeing as you were already a hundred years old when you started sleeping with him,' Leon said with a sneer.

'Oh, you're a delight, aren't you?' she replied. 'I don't know how you ever got through Archie's door in the first place.'

'Wait a minute,' Tyler said, turning on Leon. 'Everything we did, taking the money, it was always led by you. You started it, you kept increasing the stakes, you controlled all of it.'

'That's right,' Breakfast said, joining him. 'Did you rope us into this just so you could get revenge on your secret dad for abandoning you?'

'If I did, which I didn't, last time I checked you two did very well out of it until we got caught. Excuse me, what the hell are you doing?'

This last comment was addressed to Noah, who had moved across the room and was now staring right into Leon's face, barely inches away.

'Oh sorry, I'm just examining you all, seeing which of you look the most like him.'

As bizarrely as Noah was acting on this, that was a really good point. The three men couldn't physically be more different: short, sour- faced Leon, tall, lanky Breakfast and strapping, muscly Tyler. Yet none of them seemed obviously related to Trent.

But, if his latest revelation was to be believed, one of them had to be. That didn't necessarily make them the killer, though. I said as much. 'Whoever it is, the police will find you anyway. If you're not the killer, you should come forward first and be one step ahead ready to prove your innocence. Being his secret son doesn't make you his murderer. In fact, you're less likely to have killed your father.'

Silence filled the room as everyone considered my

words.

'Look, I took a few quid off him but I'm not his son, or the killer,' Breakfast said.

'Same,' Leon said. 'As if I'd be related to that scumbag.'

'Same,' Tyler agreed, before flexing his muscles with a grin. 'And no offense to any other family members, but there's not exactly a family resemblance, is there?'

'One of you has to be,' Beryl said.

'Why, just because that old goat Trent said so?' Leon snapped.

'Let's have some respect for my deceased brother please.'

'Why? Everyone here hates him, dead or alive. You can't trust the old fossil as far as you can throw him. Why should we believe he has a son, just because he said he has?'

I don't know if it was Leon's wording, but something clicked as he said that. Archie Trent had given us a riddle and I knew the solution.

'He didn't say he has a son,' I said. 'He said he *had* a son.'

'Yes, because he's dead, so he used the past tense,' Noah said, not mincing his words in referring to the deceased.

'But he used the present tense just before that. *There's something about me none of you know. I had a son*. So he definitely meant to say that deliberately.'

'But then he said they're in his room,' Pierce said. 'So, he can't mean that the son died.'

'Oh, they are in this room,' I replied. As subtly as I could, I looked at the person concerned. But I didn't want to be the one to reveal them; the information was too delicate.

I didn't have to wait for long. The person stepped forward and spoke. 'It was me. I was his son.'

It was Charley, the hotel manager.

12

'I'm a transgender woman. My dad disowned me for a long time.' Charley had the attention of the whole room as she spoke.

'How is that possible?' Pierce Trent asked. 'How did I not know about you?'

'Remember, you and your brother didn't speak for twenty years. I didn't know about you either, my dad brought me up all over Europe. By the time I found out about you, he'd already disowned me.'

'That's terrible,' Fiona said in sympathy.

'I was a bit older than you are now, about 18,' Charley continued, addressing Nat. 'I'd stuck to my guns for two years, telling my dad that I knew I was a woman deep down. His old-fashioned, ignorant brain just couldn't cope with it. He gave me an ultimatum: either I dropped it, or he disowned me.'

I thought Nat, identifying as non-binary and close to their uncle, may have been upset at this revelation, but they didn't show it.

'But you worked for him, how did that come about?' Fiona asked.

'I contacted him several times in my mid to late twenties. By then, I'd done alright by myself; I was happy and my career had gone okay as a hotel manager. He still didn't want to know, but I wouldn't let it drop. Even when he'd been linked to transphobic comments in the press, I didn't want to give up on him. Eventually, he reached out professionally. He offered me the job managing his Brighton hotel. He thought of it as an olive branch, but said he couldn't accept me personally. I thought it would be enough, or that eventually he'd come round, but it wasn't and he didn't. The final straw came when he said he'd accept me if I considered gender identity conversion therapy. So I walked away.'

'That's terrible,' Wendy Trent said. I saw her glance over at Nat, who shared a split second look with their mum before turning away.

'You should have come to me,' Pierce said.

She looked at him for a moment. 'Thank you. I should say, I do have a loving family on my mum's side. And I only really knew you from the press and the less than kind things my father said about you over the years.'

'You should have gone to the press yourself and exposed him,' Wendy said.

'I'm not sure about that,' Pierce said in reply to his wife, clearly thinking about the impact on his own career.

'So why are you here now? Was he blackmailing you too?' Wendy asked.

'Not at all. We were actually on good terms for the last year or so. He got back in touch, apologising profusely, saying he understood now. I never knew what changed his mind.'

'I do,' Pierce said. 'That would have been about the time Nat came out as non-binary. My brother, despite his faults, has always been a great uncle to Nat. Utterly dotes on them. I think it must have taken Nat's journey to understand yours.'

Nat looked uncomfortable, staring down at the floor, while Charley looked ready to explode. When she eventually spoke, it was clipped and calculated, anger brimming under every word.

'You mean to tell me, that for nearly 20 years my own dad has rejected me because of who I am, then suddenly changed his mind just because his beloved niece decides they're non-binary? But he couldn't accept his own daughter for all that time?'

'Technically, *niece* implies a female gender so you can't say that.'

'Not now,' Pierce whispered to his wife.

'So, that's it. That's why you killed your dad,' Leon said in a smug tone.

Charley looked puzzled. 'Wait, what? Yes, I've admitted he's my dad, but I didn't kill him.'

'I thought all of that was your killer confession,' Noah said.

'Confessing to being his daughter, not to murdering him. You have to believe me!'

'I believe you,' I said. 'Charley's not the killer. But I know who is.'

I paused and looked at the murderer; they looked

back at me defiantly, daring me to say their name. So I did.

'Pierce and Wendy, I'm sorry you have to hear this. But it's Nat. Nat is the killer.'

13

I'd already worked out that Archie Trent had an accomplice in setting up this whole charade.

The swapped invites, different to the ones the staff had seen. The locked room, the perfectly timed screen announcements from Archie himself. There was no way he could rely on coincidence to time his appearances as effectively as he could. Someone must have been doing that for him. And there was the *almost everyone.*

We'd then worked out that he was terminally ill, but it stood to reason that the helper must have known this to agree to helping him die in this way, which also suggested that it was someone close to him.

We knew that Charley now fell into this category following their reconciliation, but how would he have convinced her to go along with such an insane scheme? It had to be someone more naïve than that, someone younger.

And there was only one other person who seemed to be close to him.

Then, if the person was showing us the video clips at set times, they had to have the remote control on their person still, or had the opportunity to get rid of it. An opportunity like creating an argument and storming off to the balcony by themselves, where they could throw it away from twelve storeys high.

But, if this person was now the killer, something must have happened to move their allegiance away from Archie Trent and see him in a new light. Something that made them turn the tables on him and do the deed themselves.

Something like discovering the truth about Trent's bigotry, and finding out that he'd rejected his own daughter for years over their gender: an issue that now affected the killer themselves.

Nat had barely batted an eyelid when their parents had discussed Archie's transphobia earlier, and had looked uncomfortable – but not surprised – when Charley's secret was revealed, even at the horrific mention of conversion therapy. Was this because it wasn't a surprise? Did Nat know this already?

All of this was only a theory, a possibility: but as I explained it out loud, it all seemed to fit together. Didn't it?

Nat held eye contact with me defiantly, not taking their eyes off me.

'No, it's not true,' Wendy Trent said with conviction. Everyone stared at her, including her husband, who I noticed looked a lot more shocked at my theory than Wendy herself did. 'Nat isn't the murderer… I am.'

I've always had a problem with my confidence. Even though I'd had such incredible experiences over the last year or two, solving several murders successfully, I had to remember that I was an amateur. Maybe I was above my station and needed to remember my place.

My mind was whirring as I calculated my success rate of guesses so far today. I'd successfully worked out that Charley was Archie's son before gender reassignment. I knew that Leon, Tyler and Breakfast were hiding something together. I'd realised that Archie had Nat helping him set all of this up. I thought I'd worked out she was also the murderer, but now that seemed in doubt. Maybe I'd failed the challenge Archie had set for me.

Pierce moved away from Wendy and stood next to me. 'Darling, what are you saying?'

'I'm saying that I killed your brother, and I take full responsibility. Nat didn't do it.'

'Mum, stop trying to protect me! You can't keep wrapping me in cotton wool. You fuss so much about people getting my pronouns wrong. You didn't tell me that Uncle Archie was transphobic. And you didn't tell me he was…' Instead of finishing her sentence, she looked away, with a tear in her eye. 'Anyway, it doesn't matter now. Because, yes, I killed him. I killed him!'

'Sweetheart, you don't know what you're saying, you don't know what you've done. You don't know that…' Pierce trailed off, not completing his sentence

But Nat was straight there to finish the sentence

for him. 'That Uncle Archie is my real father? Yes, I know. I argued with Mum about it earlier today, right before I killed him.'

14

Nat turned to Noah. 'Your voice recorder on your phone will still work? Even with the signal blocked?'

Noah nodded enthusiastically.

'I've always trusted you. I want you to record me please. I want a record of what I'm about to say.'

Noah nodded and reached for his phone, while Wendy pleaded. 'Don't do this, Nat, please. I'll say it's me. Please. I'm sure these people will go along with it.'

'No, we won't,' Charley said as Beryl put an arm round her. Her heart must have been breaking. We'd found her dad's body today, and she'd been outed as his transgender daughter, right before she'd discovered a secret sibling who was now the killer.

'I won't let you do that anyway, Mum,' Nat said. 'Noah, start recording please.'

Pierce took his wife's hand as Nat began to speak.

'My name is Nat Trent and I hereby confess to Archie Trent's murder. I also want to confirm that nobody else in this room is in any danger.'

I noticed a visible relief in a terrified Tyler, the so-called alpha male lifeguard, as Nat continued.

'Everything that Edward Crisp guessed is right. My uncle and I have always been close. Even when him and my dad weren't speaking. Which I never understood, though I do now.

'I was the only person who knew that he was terminally ill. A rare type of cancer that only shows symptoms right near the end. He said I was the only person he could trust.' Charley and Pierce both looked hurt. 'And when he asked me to help him with his project, I couldn't say no. He'd always been so kind to me and accepting of my non-binary status. He got it so much more than Mum and Dad. Or so I thought. Looking back, I see now how many times he tried to tell me it was just a phase.'

I saw the bitterness in their eyes as they continued. 'I honestly thought it was just a murder mystery game at first. I only found out earlier today that it was real, when I came to help him set it up. He told me that he wanted to go out with a bang, on his terms, and that he wanted revenge on some old employees who'd wronged him. Every time I kept asking why Mum and Dad were there, he kept saying he'd get to that later.'

Wendy collapsed on her husband's shoulder as Nat continued. 'He told me one by one, as we wrote the letters, what each person had done to him, and why he'd blackmailed them. Until he got to you, Charley.'

They shared a look before Charley spoke in a quiet, uncertain voice. 'What did he say about me?'

'That he loved you very much. But, that... but, that you'd caused him a lot of pain with what he called your *choices*. That learning about my non-binary status had allowed him to accept you, but he wished it was different, and it was too late. But that it wasn't too late for me.'

Charley's tone changed completely. 'What do you mean, not too late for you? What did he say?'

'Gender therapy. And not above board, NHS backed therapy like GIDS, that would help me come to terms with being non-binary. Someone private he knew, probably something dodgy like the conversion therapy he offered you.'

Charley shuddered with rage. 'Disgusting. I'm so sorry.'

'After giving him a major telling off for how he treated you, I started asking him why was he so bothered about what I did. That he was your dad, but he was only my uncle. So, that's when he said it was time to tell me about Mum and Dad's secret.'

'That he was your biological father,' Pierce said. 'Nat, I'm so sorry.'

'I was filled with so much anger. I couldn't control it. I stormed out and phoned Mum, and she confirmed everything. We had a massive row and I went back to confront Uncle Archie. When I got back here, he was sitting in his deckchair, like he would be later, ready for one of you to kill him. And then, I saw the daggers waiting to be sent to each of you with your letter. Before I knew it, I picked up one of the daggers… and all that rage, all those years of not knowing… what he'd done to you, Charley, and to my mum and dad… I… I…'

There were no more words now, just wailing, as Nat collapsed on the floor in tears. Wendy threw her arms around them as she too fell to the floor. Everyone else looked on in stunned silence. Charley looked absolutely floored.

Even Noah was silent. Until he wasn't. 'I don't understand, if you'd already killed him, it was you who sent out the invites and daggers. And you still played Mr Trent's clips like he'd planned. Why did you do that?'

I'd had the same thought but wasn't going to ask. I had an idea of the answer.

'Once I calmed down, I panicked. I thought if I went through with his plan, someone else here would get the blame.'

'Me?' Charley asked, her voice raised. 'Was that your plan? Take my dad away and frame me for it.'

'No, not you. I wouldn't. I have so much respect for you and what you went through. What you've done and the person you are, is so brave. You're awesome.'

'Forgive me if I don't return the compliment,' Charley said bitterly.

Nat looked directly at her now. 'And do you know what the funny thing is? I'm not like you. I've been non-binary for less than a year. Who knows, it might actually just be a phase for me, like he said. My situation is nothing like yours, all we have in common is a rotten dad. This had nothing to do with gender. That's not why I did it.'

'Why, then?' Pierce asked sharply. 'Why did you wreck your life and everything you had ahead of you? Why did you do it?'

'Dad, don't you get it? What he did to you and Mum, blackmailing you, then thinking he could be the knight in shining armour on his death bed. He never cared about me, not truly. He tried to break up our family. And I saw red.'

'And you killed my father,' Charley said. 'Whatever the reason, you're still a murderer. You'll have to live with that for the rest of your life.'

15

'Look at him over there, Edward. Is he alright?'

We were back at the pub later that evening after bringing Noah home. The police had arrived soon after Nat's confession and they gave themselves up straight away, without incident. They'd taken initial statements from us all and were likely to follow up tomorrow, including mentions of counselling, but for now we'd been free to go. I was dreading tomorrow's call from DI Appleby, the senior detective who was my old school bully, who would want to know how I'd ended up at the centre of a major murder case again.

Fiona and I had just finished telling Mum the whole story and she'd finally left us to go serve a customer, when we'd noticed Noah sitting on his own across the pub with an orange juice, looking unusually sad and thoughtful.

It had been a hard experience: sad, frightening, unsettling. It would take us all time to adjust, but it was easy to forget with Noah's eternal optimism that he might struggle too.

'Let's go over to him,' I said as I nudged Fiona and grabbed my drink. We reached Noah's table, and for maybe the first time ever, he didn't greet us first. Instead he just stared at his drink, barely registering that we'd sat down.

'You okay, Noah?' I asked gently.

He stayed focused on his orange juice as he answered. 'They took my phone for evidence, I don't know when I'll get it back. Not that I need it for much anyway.'

This wasn't like Noah. 'What do you mean?'

'I didn't do anything useful up there today. We used my phone to record Nat's confession and that's it. I was useless. I'd be a useless police detective.'

I considered his words. 'Noah, maybe you weren't as involved in that as you usually are, but it was a very unusual situation. We were all forced into that room with a murderer for an hour, none of us knew what to do.'

'You did, you solved the murder.' He looked at his juice again sadly. 'I guess I just miss us being a team.'

Fiona looked like she was ready to speak but she didn't, instead nodding for me to carry on. So I did. 'Noah, I was forced to help in that case today. And in the other murders, we've just got roped into being involved. But you have to remember, it's not our job to solve murders. We're amateurs.'

He looked crestfallen. 'We are?'

'Yes. But the difference is, you're not even 18 yet. You can do anything you want to. If you want to go and be a real police detective, go and do it.'

'But don't forget you'd also be a great journalist,' Fiona said. 'You claimed you didn't do anything useful today but Nat picked *you* to record the confession statement. That's because they trusted you to do it.'

'Is it *they* still or is it *she* again now?' he asked in reply. 'Nat said at the end they might not even stay non-binary anyway.'

'See, that's how your brain works, you question everything. That's the make of a great journalist. Or detective. Whatever you want to be,' Fiona said.

'You really think so?' he asked before Fiona nodded. 'Thank you. I'm off to do some career research, I'll use my laptop upstairs.'

He hugged us both and we watched him bound across to the door of the flat, the usual spring back in his step.

'Well done, you,' I said as I clinked Fiona's glass.

'And you,' she replied. 'Though you were wrong about one thing. You said the difference is Noah can go do anything he wants to. But so can you.'

I put my hand on hers and enjoyed the warm feel of it. 'Thank you. But I don't want to be a detective. And after tonight, I don't want to be involved in any more murder cases. I'm done with it.'

I felt her squeeze my hand. 'It was a difficult one today, wasn't it? Poor Charley. And the poor Trents seeing their daughter confess to murder. And poor Archie himself, I guess. He was the murder victim.'

This struck a nerve. That's exactly why I didn't want to be involved in these cases. Everything was just too grey. Archie Trent was brutally murdered and we should feel sorry for him; like Fiona said, he's the murder victim. However, he did horrific things to so many people. For example, a teenage girl was driven to murder because of him. But she'd made that choice and murder is never justified, ever.

I was sick of thinking like this. Policemen, detectives and similar professions were trained and given support to deal with these traumatic, complicated situations: I wasn't.

I first fell in love with fictional murder mysteries because they were an escape from reality. But these real life cases were the opposite: the reality was grim.

I didn't voice any of this, but it was as if Fiona read my mind. 'If you want to stay away from real murder cases and stick to your fictional murder mysteries, you have my blessing.'

'Thank you.' I was so lucky to have her.

'But I don't just mean reading them. I mean writing them.'

'What do you mean?'

'Edward, like I said, you can do anything. You've told me before about your novel when you were younger. You're clearly brilliant at whatever you put your mind to, so I think you'd be a brilliant novelist. I think it's fine to give it a go.'

Something about what she said felt right. 'You know what? I think you might have a point.'

EDWARD AND NOAH WILL RETURN SOON IN THE FULL NOVEL, TEN GREEN BOTTLES.

Acknowledgments

It's been a while, hasn't it? I'm delighted to bring Edward, Noah and company back for their fifth adventure. This one, like *The Mystery Of Jackson King* earlier in the series, is a shorter installment than my full novels but I do enjoy writing these novella length stories; I hope you enjoy them too. Next stop, Ten Green Bottles!

I want to start by mentioning my amazing ARC and proof reading team: Charlotte, Hannah, Helen, Karen, Kerry, Lisa, Michelle, Robyn, Tia and Zoe. Thank you for all the silly errors you spotted (Noah's changing age, writing TIME ready to decide an exact time later, to name a couple!), typos and all the amazing insight and feedback each of you gave to this book. In return, I promise I won't kill off your favourites (or will I?).

Thanks to my paperback designer, Marion, my ad designer, Jon, and my best author friends, Ben and Helen – so fantastic to finally meet in person at the SPS conference!

Of course, thanks to all of my lovely readers and social media followers. My interactions with each of you are one of my favourite things about being an author over the last two years. Thank you for taking my books and characters into your hearts.

Massive thanks, as ever, to Samantha Brownley and all the admins and readers at UK Crime Book Club who have given me such fantastic support, and Donna Morfett at Donna's Interviews Reviews and Giveaways. These two Facebook groups are such an amazing help to authors (and great for readers, too!).

Love and thanks as always to Mum and Dad, and all my family, for your love and support. And all my friends, north and south, for your friendship.

Last but not least, Graeme, thank you for being there for me always. The kindest and best man I know.

Printed in Great Britain
by Amazon